Dear mouse friends,
Welcome to the world of

Geronimo Stilton

THE RODENT'S GAZETTE
EDITORIAL STAFF

Geronimo Stilton
A learned and brainy
mouse; editor of
The Rodent's Gazette

Thea Stilton
Geronimo's sister and
special correspondent at
The Rodent's Gazette

Trap Stilton
An awful joker;
Geronimo's cousin and
owner of the store
Cheap Junk for Less

Benjamin Stilton
A sweet and loving
nine-year-old mouse;
Geronimo's favorite
nephew

Geronimo Stilton

HAPPY BIRTHDAY, GERONIMO!

Scholastic Inc.

The publisher does not have any control over and does not assume any responsibility for author or third-party websites or their content.

GERONIMO STILTON names, characters, and related indicia are copyright, trademark, and exclusive license of Atlantyca S.p.A. All rights reserved. The moral right of the author has been asserted. Based on an original idea by Elisabetta Dami. geronimostilton.com

Published by Scholastic Inc., *Publishers since 1920*, 557 Broadway, New York, NY 10012. SCHOLASTIC and associated logos are trademarks and/or registered trademarks of Scholastic Inc.

Stilton is the name of a famous English cheese. It is a registered trademark of the Stilton Cheese Makers' Association.

This book is a work of fiction. Names, characters, places, and incidents are either the product of the author's imagination or are used fictitiously, and any resemblance to actual persons, living or dead, business establishments, events, or locales is entirely coincidental.

ISBN 978-1-338-58753-1

Text by Geronimo Stilton
Original title *Comlpleanno . . . con mistero!*
Art director: Iacopo Bruno
Cover by Roberto Ronchi and Alessandro Muscillo
Illustrations by Danilo Loizedda, Antonio Campo, and Daria Cerchi
Graphic designer: Laura Dal Maso / theWorldofDOT
Graphics by Michela Battaglin

Special thanks to Tracey West
Translated by Lidia Tramontozzi
Interior design by Kevin Callahan / BNGO Books

10 9 8 7 6 5 4 3 2   20 21 22 23 24

Printed in the U.S.A.   40

First printing 2020

HAPPY BIRTHDAY, GERONIMO!

I woke up to a chilly spring Saturday morning. Outside my window, the wind blew, whooshing off hats from rodents scampering along the streets of New Mouse City, that bustling city where I . . .

It's windy!

I'm sorry. I forgot to introduce myself. My name is Stilton, *Geronimo Stilton*. I run a newspaper called *The Rodent's Gazette*, the most famouse newspaper on Mouse Island!

I had woken up in a mouserific mood because . . . it was my **BiRTHDAY**! I quickly got ready for the day as I sang a happy tune:

"Oh, what a beautiful morn . . . Today is the day I was born . . . Today will be breezy . . . And pleasant and cheesy . . . I'm happy to say . . . That today's my birthday!"

I started off with a shower. I stepped inside the stall, lathered myself with gorgonzola-scented soap (a favorite fragrance for us rodents), but . . .

This kind of thing always happens to me!

"A nice, cheesy breakfast will make me feel better," I said.

I fixed myself a tasty meal of CHEESE toast and a yummy cup of hot chocolate. But because I was already late, I guzzled the hot chocolate all in one gulp . . . and burned my tongue!

ARGH! I'M SUCH A KLUTZ!!!

But I did not let my aching tongue dampen my spirit. After all, it was my BIRTHDAY! So, I put on my jacket, knotted my tie, opened the DOOR, and left for work.

A Cheesy Breakfast

I had a cheesy birthday breakfast, but a breakfast made with cheese is mousetastic on any day of the year!

Here are some ways to make your breakfast cheesier:

- Sprinkle cheese on your favorite cereal.

- Toast some cheese bread and top with jam.

- Whip up a cheese omelet.

- You can even eat pie for breakfast – when it's ricotta pie!

Some things that go great with cheese are:

- Fresh fruit

- Rolls and croissants

Do you know what makes a **cheesy** breakfast better? Eating it with **family** or **friends**. Good company and good food can lead to one thing: **A guaranteed cheese-tastic day!**

THE STRANGE BAMBOOZLE FAMILY

With my belly full of cheesy **BiRTHDAY** breakfast, I stepped out into the sunny morning. I was running late, and I had to move my tail! I was about to cross the street when I saw an enormouse moving van.

A strange family climbed out!

How **strange** were they? They were strange, strange, strange! Very **strange**! In fact, very, very **strange**!

They each wore a yellow lab coat, like scientists. But underneath, they wore very **colorful** clothes.

The oldest rodent had gray hair gathered up in a bun. She was **barking** at the three younger rodents.

"Listen to me, Bettina Bamboozle! Your aunt and I are in charge of this family!"

She wore three keys around her neck, and she carried a big pink handbag locked with three big padlocks. I gathered, from what Bettina had said, that the three young rodents were her *nephews*. They noticed me and began introducing themselves.

"Good morning! I am **Balencio Bamboozle!**" said the first. A red comb was tucked into his lab coat pocket.

Balencio took the comb out of his pocket and ran it through his shiny, well-oiled **fur**. Then he did a backflip!

Bettina is the overbearing aunt in charge of the family. She has two great passions: knitting and cooking! Her specialties are licorice lasagna, chocolate meat sauce, clam smoothies, and oyster tarts. Have an excuse ready if she ever invites you to dinner.

Balencio is the oldest Bamboozle brother. He works out every day and dreams of becoming a circus acrobat.

Bobo is the youngest of the Bamboozle brothers. He's a great prankster, and his secret dream is to become a circus clown!

Burton is the middle Bamboozle brother. He, too, loves the circus, but dreams of becoming a magician. In fact, he always has his wand and hat with him!

"Hello, neighbor!" Balencio said.

"I am Burton Bamboozle," said the second nephew. Curiously, he wore a magician's hat and white gloves with his lab coat. He waved his wand at me. "Hocus-pocus! Greetings, neighbor!"

"And I am Bobo Bamboozle!" said the third nephew. He wore a clown's jacket under his lab coat and a funny little straw hat on his head. He bopped a giant plastic hammer on the ground, and it made a squeaky noise. "Hee, hee, hee! Howdy, neighbor!"

I was going to say, "Good morning. My name is Geronimo Stilton. Welcome to the neighborhood!" But my tongue was still SWOLLEN from the scalding hot cocoa. So instead I whimpered,

"Mmm nmm th Grmm Stmmm. Wmm th th thmmmm!"

"What did you say, marble mouth?" Bobo asked.

I turned **red** with embarrassment! But Bettina kindly smiled at me and held out her paw.

"Hello! You must be Mr. Stilton!" she said. I nodded.

Mmm . . .

You must be Mr. Stilton!

"How nice to meet the editor of *The Rodent's Gazette*," she said.

I politely shook her paw and wanted to say, "Pleased to meet you. I hope you will be happy here!" But instead I whimpered, "*Thp th mmm. Pth wth mm hmmm!*"

She smiled and nodded to the movers. "These rodents are working so hard," she said. "I must give them a nice big tip when they are done."

DO NOT TOUCH! PROPERTY OF THE BAMBOOZLE FAMILY!

KEEP OUT!

KEEP OUT!

PAWS OFF

Mr. Stilton, Can You Help Me?

Bettina Bamboozle unlocked the three **padlocks** of her enormouse handbag.

Click, click, click!

She threw open the handbag and took out a bill.

"I have no **small** bills to tip the movers with. Can you help me, Mr. Stilton?"

Balencio spoke up: "Auntie, I think I have . . ."

"**QUIET!**" she shouted. "Only your aunt is allowed to think!" And then she bopped his head with her enormouse handbag.

Bonk!

She turned back to me and *smiled* sweetly. "Can you give me some small bills for this large one?" she asked again.

Hmmm . . .   Quiet!!!   Argh . . .

Partly because I wanted to be **NICE** to my new neighbors, and partly because I didn't want to be bonked on the head with that enormouse handbag, I agreed.

"*Thmm, mmm! Thly!*" I replied. (Translation: "Certainly, madam! Gladly!")

She handed me the MONEY, and I changed it with smaller bills.

I tucked the bill into my pocket.

I had so many questions about this **strange** family!

I couldn't ask them, because they couldn't understand me! Then Balencio **startled** me by taking a glass bottle from his pocket and thrusting it at my whiskers.

"Mr. Stilton, because you are our neighbor, we will now offer you, free of charge, a taste of our BBB!" he said. "Bamboozle Bubbly Beverage, produced and bottled exclusively by our family!"

Before I could SQUEAK, he flipped and stood on one paw. With the other paw, he poured a spoonful of BBB into my mouth!

The BBB was a GREEN liquid that tasted worse than anything I had ever consumed. It smelled as if garlic, onion, cabbage, broccoli,

rotten eggs, and fermented cheese had been brewed in a **dirty sock**! When it landed in my stomach, I could feel it *sloshing* around. *Ugh!*

The neighborhood MOSQUITOES seemed to like it. They swarmed around the beverage bottle.

Bobo Bamboozle BONKED me on the tail with his big rubber hammer, snorting,

Here we go!

Gulp!

KEEP OUT!

"This will help you digest the Bamboozle Bubbly Beverage! Hee, hee, hee!"

My wallet flew out of my pocket. When I got to my feet, Burton handed it to me.

"Here you go, neighbor," he said.

"*Thn!*" I replied, because my tongue was still hurting. (Translation: "Thanks!")

Mrs. Bamboozle stuck the gift inside my pocket: a tiny corked bottle containing a

Bamboozle Bubbly Beverage

A remedy for every mouse malady!

INGREDIENTS:
Cod liver oil, onion, garlic, cabbage juice, broccoli juice, rotten eggs, fermented cheese, molasses,
Note: This beverage is sweetened with super-concentrated poison-ivy honey, so if your tongue itches, that's why!

This delicious beverage is the only remedy you will need for anything that ails you! Frazzled fur? BBB can fix it! Droopy whiskers? BBB can fix them! Feeling sluggish after too much cheese? BBB can fix that! Our bubbly beverage is the cure for every mouse malady!

thick green liquid. In capital letters, the label read: "Bamboozle Bubbly Beverage. A remedy for every mouse malady!"

"*Gby!*" I muttered. (Translation: "Goodbye!") Then I quickly scampered away. My odd neighbors were making me very uncomfortable.

I was already very super-mega-extra late!

As I scurried away, my tummy began to rumble. Glub! Glub! Glub!

A Very,
Very, Very
Suspicious Bill!

I was glad to have an excuse to get away from the Bamboozles. The news waits for no mouse!

On my way to *The Rodent's Gazette*, I stopped at the newsstand to buy the paper, like I do every day. It's good

Very suspicious!

Huh?!

for business! I took a **bill** from my pocket and handed it to the vendor.

"This bill looks very suspicious! Where did you get it, Mr. Stilton?" he asked, holding it up in the air to get a better look.

"Im nth thr!" (Translation: "I'm not sure!")

I kept the bill, left the paper, and ran away. I was in a terrible hurry to find something that would soothe my stomach. I was wondering what could have made me so sick, I didn't even stop to think about what the vendor said about the money. My tummy rumbled again.

GLUB! GLUB! GLUB!

I decided that a cup of warm tea might help me feel better. I rushed over to the cafe and ordered a chamomile tea. But when I paid,

Simon Shakypaws squinted at the bill.

"This bill looks very, very, very suspicious. Where did you get it, Mr. Stilton?" he asked.

"Im nth thr!" (Translation: "I'm not sure!")

GLUB! **GLUB!** GLUB!

I scurried away, with my tummy rumbling. Now I was really, really late. Even so, I had to stop at the PHARMACY because I was getting a **headache**. But when I tried to pay, the pharmacist questioned me.

"This bill looks very, very, very suspicious! Where did you get it, Mr. Stilton?" she asked.

Again, I repeated, *"Im nth thr!"* (Translation: "I'm not sure!")

Now I hightailed it to the offices of *The Rodent's Gazette*, where I work.

My tummy kept rumbling:

GLUB! GLUB! GLUB!

I felt queasy. I felt crummy. I needed a

RESTROOM!

As soon as I got to my office, I SCURRIED toward the bathroom as if I were being chased by a hungry cat. My coworkers ran after me, but I locked myself in!

Someone knocked on the door. "Geronimo, we're getting ready for a SPECIAL edition of *The Rodent's Gazette*. We have **breaking news** on a story that is very, very, very strange. We need a reporter with a nose for investigation to jump on the story. *Can you do it?*"

My TONGUE finally seemed to be back to normal.

"Please ask my sister, Thea, to write the article!" I yelled through the door. "Thanks! I'm a bit busy!"

I was not feeling very well!

A VERY BAD DAY
AT THE OFFICE

I had a bad stomachache for a while. When I finally started to feel a tiny bit better, I really needed to **rest**.

I was shivering, so I put on three sweaters (yes, three!) to keep warm. And to help my tummy feel better, I drank three cups of soothing tea (yes, three!).

My birthday had gotten off to a pretty bad start, and it was all because of that *Bamboozle Bubbly*

Beverage! It really did a number on me. My new neighbors were turning out to be the absolute **worst**!

After three more hours (yes, three!), I tried to sit up. But my tummy kept grumbling. I searched in my drawers for something to take. I had stuff for a cold and stuff for bee stings and for headaches and for allergies and for scaredy-mice . . .

Finally, all the way in the back was something for upset stomachs. I took some and waited for my stomach to quiet down.

GLUB! GLUB! GLUB!

I could finally sit up straight at the end of the day—after all my coworkers had left. When evening came, I was still not feeling

well. My tummy was still rumbling. **Glub! I felt horrible!**

But I had made plans to be with my family at the swankiest restaurant in the city, the **GOLDEN CHEESE**. I didn't want to disappoint them! So, I decided to go anyway!

Feeling very depressed, I left my office and headed toward the Golden Cheese.

I was having such a rotten birthday!

My tummy hurts! Arghhh!

My tummy
still went:
Glub!
Glub!
Glub!
Glub!

THE
GOLDEN CHEESE

When I got to the restaurant, my tummy still went: **Glub! Glub! Glub!**

I scurried to the long table where my family was waiting for me.

"**Happy birthday, Geronimo!**" they all shouted.

I smiled and took a seat. **SQUEAK!** Everyone was here. Absolutely everyone! My sister, Thea. My cousin Trap. My nephew Benjamin. All my close friends.

Hmm . . . no! Wait up! One **RODENT** was missing! Where was Hercule Poirat, my childhood friend?

Hercule and I had been friends since we were little mouselings in school. He had been

With Hercule on my
3rd birthday!

With Hercule on my
5th birthday!

The Birthdays
of
Geronimo Stilton

With Hercule on
my 7th birthday!

With Hercule on my
10th birthday!

to every single one of my **BiRTHDAYS** since we had known each other. So many **HAPPY** memories!

Strangely, I did see *Madame No* seated in a corner, half-hidden behind a newspaper. She was staring at me and wearing an evil grin I did not like. **WHY?**

Madame No!

Madame No is the CEO of EGO Corp. (Enormously Gigantic Organization), a powerful company that handles a lot of real-estate deals on Mouse Island. EGO Corp. builds malls and skyscrapers and owns airlines, newspapers, and TV stations. Whenever you ask her a question, she will always answer with one word: "NO!"

Squeak! I'm Not Dr. Falsefur!

Luckily, my tummy had finally calmed down. I was able to eat all the delicious CHEESE dishes that the restaurant had prepared.

After dinner, the waiter brought out a huge BIRTHDAY CAKE for me. As I blew out the CANDLES, everyone sang:

"*Happy birthday to you!* May you eat lots of CHEESE! Happy birthday, Geronimo! Eat as much as you please!"

I was lucky to be surrounded by so many rodents who loved me!

One by one, all my friends left. In the restaurant, only a few rodents remained.

THEN THE CLOCK STRUCK MIDNIGHT!

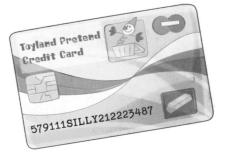

Yawning, I went to the cash register to pay the bill. I took out my **CREDIT CARD** and handed it to the restaurant manager. He looked at it and raised a furry eyebrow.

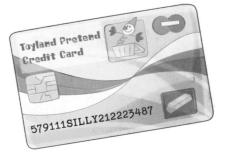

"Mr. Stilton, this says 'Toyland Pretend Credit Card'! Is this a joke?" he asked.

"I'm sorry. That's strange," I said. "I'll pay by check."

When I handed him a check, he frowned. "Are you pulling my tail?"

I looked at the **check** and gasped. The check should have read New Mouse City

Bank. Instead, it read *Pranks Bank*! Printed in the corner was a clown making a funny face!

"Er . . . don't worry. I'll pay with CASH!" I stammered.

I dug into my pocket and gave him the bill that I had tried to use to pay for my NEWSPAPER, my **tea**, and my headache MEDICINE. But as soon as I put it on the counter, he screamed, "What kind of silly bill is this?!"

I finally understood why everybody thought it was very, very, very SUSPICIOUS! I turned over the bill, and it said, *If you think this is real money . . . you're a real cheesehead!*

The restaurant manager stared at me **suspiciously**.

"Can I please see some identification?"

I took my wallet out of my pocket. "My name is *Stilton, Geronimo Stilton*, and . . ."

As soon as I opened the wallet, a squirt of water hit the manager right in the snout!

"Do you think this is funny?" he asked,

I'm sorry!

What are you doing?!

infuriated. "You tried to pay with a phony credit card! You tried to give me a bogus check with a clown's face on it! And then you gave me a counterfeit bill. You are in **BIG TROUBLE!**"

I took out my ID card. It read *Dr. Falsefur*. Instead of my photograph, there was a picture of a piece of cheese!

The manager grabbed the telephone, shouting, "I'm calling the police! The joke's on you, Dr. Falsefur!"

A waiter grabbed me by the tail so I wouldn't run off. OUCH!

A photographer was in the restaurant, and he began taking dozens of photos.

"Here's Dr. Falsefur! The sneaky mouse has been unmasked!" he cried.

And as luck would have it, two gossip reporters happened to be having dinner

that night: SAMANTHA TATTLETAIL and **Simon Squealer.** They scampered away to notify the tabloids they worked for.

"It looks like Dr. Falsefur got caught with his paws in the cookie jar!" they squealed.

Madame No chuckled happily. "Geronimo Stilton's in trouble!"

Her crew began to chant in singsong voices: "Geronimo Stilton's in trouble!"

Ha, ha, ha!

My family and friends were outside the restaurant, waiting for me. I was all alone and in a big mess . . .

My birthday was turning into a **NIGHTMARE!**

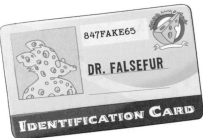

"I'm an honest mouse!" I explained to the manager. "I'd never try to pay with **phony money**. Squeak! I'm not *Dr. Falsefur*!"

That's when I heard a loud voice behind me.

"**Leave that mouse alone!** I'll vouch for him!"

A VERY, VERY, VERY STRANGE CASE!

I turned and saw a familiar face: Hercule Poirat, my detective friend! I **hugged** him with relief!

"Hercule, please explain that I'm a good mouse!" I begged.

He told the manager that I was the editor of *The Rodent's Gazette* and assured him I was an honest mouse. Then he paid the bill with his own credit card.

After he had paid, he rummaged through the pockets of his yellow trench coat and took out a banana. He peeled it and offered it to me.

"Nibble on a banana, Geronimo. You look PALE. You had a bad day, huh?" he asked.

I nodded.

"Don't worry," Hercule said. "I will figure out this very, very, very strange *mystery*!"

"I'm sorry, Mr. Stilton," the manager interrupted. "All of New Mouse City has been talking about the **FAKE MONEY** that is being circulated everywhere. I was very worried."

He pointed to the special edition of *The Rodent's Gazette*. The headline read: "**Very, Very, Very Strange Bills in New Mouse City!**" I didn't know about it because I had been sick all day!

That's why . . .

"I'm sorry I was late to your BiRTHDAY party, Geronimo," Hercule said as we left the restaurant. "I have been busy trying to solve this mystery. I am trying to track down where the FAKE BILLS are coming from. Do you remember where you got yours from, Geronimo?"

My whiskers twitched as I tried to remember. "My memory is as holey as Swiss cheese today," I said. "After my new neighbors gave me a taste of the stinky drink they make, I was sick all day. I could have gotten that FAKE BILL anywhere."

"And how did that Dr. Falsefur ID card get into your wallet?" he asked.

I scratched my head. "Well, it's not even my wallet. It's a fake. Maybe *Madame No* planted it there. She seemed awfully happy to see me in trouble."

"Interesting," Hercule said. "This mystery is getting *stranger* and *stranger*."

"*Good luck* solving it, Hercule," I said. "I am very tired from my long, strange birthday. I need to get home."

"You have to help me solve this mystery!" Hercule said. "We are a great team, Geronimo. Like *cheese and crackers*!"

How could I say no to my best friend? "Okay, I'll do it."

Hercule jumped to his feet. "Excellent! To the *Bananamobile*!"

OFF IN THE BANANAMOBILE!

We raced outside and hopped into Hercule's Bananamobile. He revved the engine, and we zoomed off.

The Bananamobile is the strangest car ever! It is yellow, with a yellow steering wheel. The floor mats and seats have banana patterns on them. The car has a small fridge filled with fresh bananas, banana juice, banana fruit salad, banana candy, and banana chewing gum! Thanks to a "banana-fresh" deodorizer, the car always smells like RIPE BANANAS.

Hercule turned on the radio, and his favorite song blared from the speakers: "Banana Feeling" by the Banana Boys.

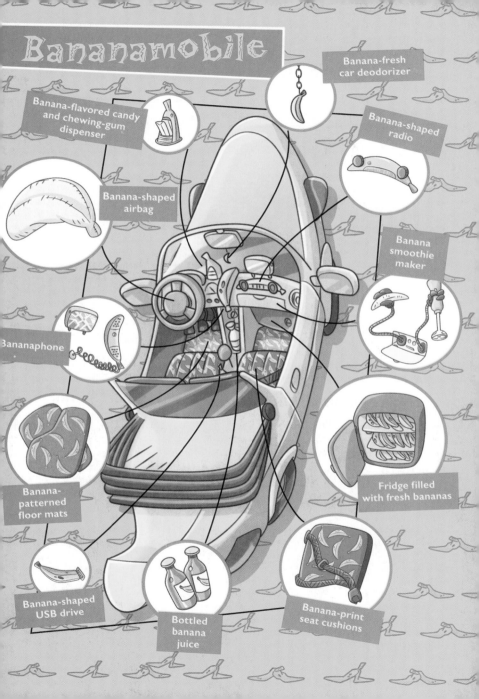

"Dr. Falsefur, Hercule and Geronimo are coming for you!" he cried.

Suddenly, he stopped the car and examined the **fake bills** that he had collected.

HERCULE AND GERONIMO ARE ON THE CASE!

"Hmm," he said. "Hundreds of **phony** bills have popped up around the city. It must have taken a big printing press to make them."

"Printing presses are **noisy**, too," I said.

"Exactly!" Hercule agreed. "So let's begin our search by looking at all of the noisy, big buildings in New Mouse City."

We drove around the entire **night**, checking out every warehouse in the city. We didn't find the **phony-money** makers in any of them. When the sun rose, I was falling asleep. But Hercule looked as fresh as a young cheese.

"Aren't you tired?" I asked.

"I feel great," he answered. "But you look paler than **MOZZARELLA**!"

"I am exhausted!" I replied.

"I know exactly what you need to put some pep in your step," Hercule said. "You need a BANANA BOOST!"

He pushed a button near the steering wheel and a mechanical arm popped out in front of me, holding a list of smoothies. A tiny metallic voice asked me, "What kind of smoothie would you like, Mr. Stilton?"

Hercule elbowed me and whispered, "Pick number TWELVE. It's the best!"

"Uhm, number twelve, please!"

BANANAS FOR BANANAS!

Bananas are high in potassium, a mineral that helps keep your heart healthy. They are rich in fiber, which helps you digest the food you eat. And they contain vitamin B6, which can help keep your mind sharp! That is why Hercule loves them.

1 The **MACHINE** handed me a glass and a menu . . . **bzzzzz**!

2 **PLUCK, PLUCK!** It quickly peeled a banana and **STUCK** it inside the glass.

3 It whipped the banana . . . whirrrrrr!

4 Added **milk** . . . splash!

5 Dropped in a **SLICE** of lemon . . . *plip*!

6 And plopped in **THREE** strawberries . . . PLOP, PLOP, PLOP!

"Drink it up!" Hercule urged me. "It's good for you! Hercule Poirat says so!"

I brought the glass to my lips . . . but Hercule suddenly stepped on the gas! The

smoothie splashed on my **WHISKERS**! I crashed against the door. The bottle of *Bamboozle Bubbly Beverage* broke inside my pocket and soaked my pants.

I was a total **mess**!

So, with my **WHISKERS** full of smoothie and my pants soaked with *smelly green beverage*, I continued the investigation

Hee, hee, hee!

with Hercule. Flies followed me wherever we went, because the BBB smelled so bad!

We hadn't found the printing press, so we tried another tactic. We decided to question all the rodents who (like me), had fallen victim to *Dr. Falsefur* . . .

THE HUNT FOR DR. FALSEFUR

"We'll pay a little visit to the other victims of **Dr. Falsefur**," Hercule announced.

He adjusted his seat and accidentally squashed my tail.

"**Ooouch!**" I yelled.

He thrust a banana fruit salad into my right paw. "You need another **BANANA BOOST**, Geronimo!" he said. "Eat this right now! It's got honey and lemon for an extra kick!"

He shoved a map of New Mouse City into my left paw.

"I marked this **MAP** with all the places where this swindler has dumped any **funny money**," Hercule told me.

He stepped on the gas. We were going so fast that:

1. My tail got **STUCK** between the seats.

2. The fruit salad **splattered** all over my jacket. The honey in it was sticky, and the lemon stung my eyes!

3. The map **flapped** like crazy and got stuck on my snout!

"**Aaaarghhh!**" I yelled.

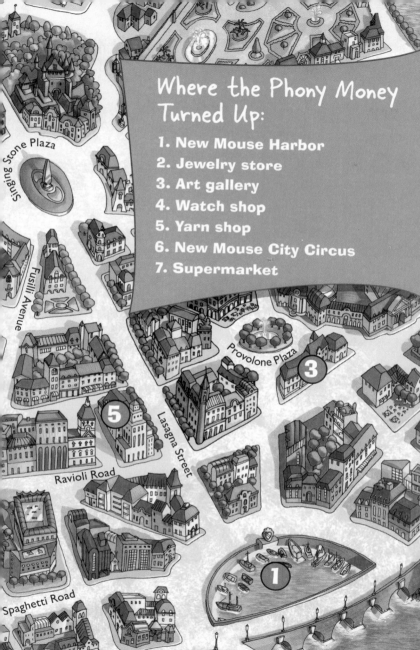

Where the Phony Money Turned Up:

1. **New Mouse Harbor**
2. **Jewelry store**
3. **Art gallery**
4. **Watch shop**
5. **Yarn shop**
6. **New Mouse City Circus**
7. **Supermarket**

Singing Stone Plaza

Fusilli Avenue

Provolone Plaza

Lasagna Street

Ravioli Road

Spaghetti Road

Hercule went even *faster*.

"You're wide awake now, aren't you, Geronimo?" he called out over the roaring engine. "**EXCELLENT!** First stop: New Mouse Harbor!"

We headed toward the **SEA RODENT TAVERN**, a hangout for sailors. We walked in and the owner, Henry Herring, scurried toward us.

"Yesterday, a rodent came in and bought all the supplies in the warehouse," he told us. "He said he needed them for a long **sea** voyage. Instead of paying by check, he paid in cash. When I took the bills to the bank, I was told they were fake."

He BURST out crying. "Now my business is in trouble. I may have to close my tavern!"

While he was talking, I noticed a green stain next to the cash register and asked about it. "Where did this come from?"

All That Glitters

"Now that I think of it, Mr. Stilton, the bills were stained with a strange, sticky green substance," Herring remembered.

After the tavern, we headed to the jewelry store, **All That Glitters**. We met with the owner, Joy Jewelrat, who opened a drawer and showed us a pile of money.

"A mouse came in and bought a very expensive gold diamond necklace," Joy explained. "She paid me with these bills! After she left, I realized they were **phony**.

I gave her that necklace for **NOTHING**!"

"She?" I asked. "So it was a female mouse who gave you the **phony** money?"

Jewel nodded. "Yes," she replied. "She wore pink sunglasses and carried big pink handbag."

Pink handbag? Why did that sound familiar to me? I wondered.

"This is a CLUE!" Hercule exclaimed. "It

This is what happened . . .

I'll take that!

sounds like we are dealing with a whole team of crooks, not just one!"

Next we went to the *Gallery of Modern Mice*. The most famous artists on Mouse Island display their art there. The owner of the gallery, Art Paintpaws, rushed up to us when we arrived.

"I feel like such a cheeseface!" he blurted out. "This is what happened: We put a painting by **Vincent van Gouda** on the auction block. The room was **packed** with rodents eager to bid on it. But one rodent kept **outbidding** everyone else!"

"A male rodent?" Hercule asked.

"Yes, a very nervous male rodent," Art replied. "We gave him the painting and he left in a **hurry**. Only then did I realize that he had paid me with FAKE MONEY! He dropped this when he left."

Art held up a white glove.

HMMM, IT REMINDED ME OF SOMEONE ... WHO?

Hercule frowned. "We have to stop Dr. Falsefur. This rodent—or rodents—has **HURT** so many in New Mouse City. On to the next stop!"

We entered the **TICKTOCK WATCH SHOP**. The owners, Lance and Lena Timeteller, looked hopeful when they saw us.

"Did you catch him? Do you know who Dr. Falsefur is?"

"Not yet," Hercule apologized. "But soon. We will **crack** this case soon."

Lance sighed. "They bought a very expensive gold pocket watch from us, and they paid with **PHONY** bills." He sighed.

"They?" Hercule asked. "More than one mouse?"

Lena nodded. "There were *four* of them, and they quarreled the whole time."

HMM, WHO DID THAT DESCRIPTION REMIND ME OF?

This is what happened . . .

Perfect!

You keep quiet!

Our next stop was ᥡarn Paradiᴄe.

"Weird," Hercule said. "I can understand buying gold and art, but why would crooks want a bunch of yarn?"

An elderly rodent ran the tiny, old-fashioned shop. She was sitting by the counter, knitting.

"I remember the rodent who paid with the fake money," she squeaked. "She **BOUGHT** quite a lot of yarn, and she only wanted pink!"

"Pink?" I asked.

"Yes, pink," the owner replied. "She said she needed to knit herself a coat to match her pink bag."

Hercule looked at his notes. "Pink bag. That sounds like the rodent who stole the necklace at the jewelry store. I see a pattern here!"

Hmm, there was something familiar about all this.

MY SWISS-CHEESE MEMORY WAS STARTING TO RECOVER!

This is what happened . . .

Here you go!

We said good-bye, and Hercule checked the map. "Our next stop is the New Mouse City Circus!" he announced.

At the circus ticket window, the cashier confirmed that four rodents had bought tickets with FAKE BILLS. He added that they had really enjoyed the show.

"They clapped and laughed and cheered louder than anyone else," he reported. "They especially liked the ACROBATS, the magician's act, and the clowns. They seemed to really LOVE the clowns!"

SOMETHING ELSE REMINDED ME OF A CIRCUS YESTERDAY . . .

This is what happened . . .

I had an idea who might be behind all the fake money. But I didn't want to say anything without more **proof**.

Hercule and I went to the last stop—the **SUPERMARKET**.

The cashier told us that four rodents had spent an enormouse amount of the fake money on an unusual combination of ingredients: garlic, onions, broccoli, cabbage, and molasses.

CRACKING THE CASE

I turned to Hercule. "I think I've **cracked the case!**"

"Really, Geronimo?" Hercule asked. "Do you know who **Dr. Falsefur** is?"

"I think I do," I replied. "You were **right**, Hercule. Dr. Falsefur is not one single rodent. It's a team of **FOUR RODENTS**. Four rodents who are my new neighbors: the **Bamboozles**!"

"Excellent!" Hercule cried. "But how did you figure it out?"

"There are four members of the family," I said. "The three nephews all wore **circus** outfits under their lab coats. When we met, Balencio did a backflip, like an acrobat. Burton waved his wand, like a magician.

And Bobo bopped me on the head, like a clown."

Hercule nodded. "They seem to like the circus!"

"The aunt, Bettina, asked me if I could change a **LARGE BiLL** for her," I went on. "So that's probably where I got the **funny money**. And then Bobo bopped me on the head again, and I dropped my wallet! I bet that's when they switched my wallet for the one with the fake ID. And they were loading dozens of **heavy** crates into their new house."

"Crates that could have held *printing* equipment," my friend concluded.

"How do we **PROVE** that they are guilty?" I asked.

"We'll catch them in the act!" Hercule cried. "To the Bananamobile!"

All the clues for this strange case

1 I remembered that my wallet fell in front of Burton . . .

2 The movers unloaded mysterious crates . . .

KEEP OUT!

3 Bettina Bamboozle insisted that I make change for her large bill . . .

(4) At the tavern, there was a green stain by the cash register . . .

(5) In the jewelry store, the thief carried a pink handbag . . .

At the art gallery, the thief dropped a white glove . . .

(6)

(7) In the watch showroom, the thieves were always quarreling . . .

The thief had bought pink yarn . . .

(8)

The thieves seemed to love the circus . . .

(9)

Garlic, onions, broccoli, cabbage, and molasses are all ingredients in BBB!

(10)

We jumped into the car. Hercule stuck a F L A S H I N G red light on the hood and turned on the SIREN. The New Mouse City police had allowed him to use it in cases such as this.

Driving at **mousestastic** speed, we were at my house before I could squeak *banana*. I immediately saw a moving van

parked (again!), in front of the neighboring house. And (again!!) the **movers** were hard at work. And (again!!!) they were moving enormouse crates. But this time, they were moving them **out** of the house—not into the house.

As soon as the three Bamboozle nephews saw me, they squeaked, "Good morning, Mr.

Step on it, Hercule!

Stilton. We have to move because —"

Bettina Bamboozle did not let them finish. She **bonked** each of them on the *head* with her huge handbag.

"**Zip it**, the three of you! Let me do the talking!" Bettina barked.

Then she turned toward Hercule and

me and squeaked with a voice as sweet as honey, "Ooh, good morning, Mr. Stilton! We have to move **SUDDENLY** because I have **URGENT** business to attend to in another city."

"Is that so?" Hercule replied nonchalantly. "What kind of business?"

She frowned. "**Bamboozle** business, that's what! It's nobody's business but our own."

She turned to the three nephews. "Bamboozle nephews, forward march!" she commanded.

The three rodents scurried toward the moving van.

Then she turned to the movers. "And you! Load up the van with the machines we need to make the *Bamboozle Bubbly Beverage!*"

MYSTERY SOLVED!

Hercule stepped in front of Bettina and shook his head.

"You say that these crates hold the machines to make your **beverage**," he said. "But I bet that's not true."

"**NONSENSE!**" Bettina replied.

Hercule *grabbed* one side of the crate. "Let me see!"

Heave ho!

Pull!

Inside the van!

"Let go of that crate!" Bettina yelled. "It goes inside the van!"

"I must **investigate**! Leave it outside!" Hercule demanded.

Bettina grabbed the other side of the crate. A tug-of-war began to gain control of it. The Bamboozle nephews helped their aunt. I helped Hercule. And one of the poor movers was stuck in the middle.

"Outside or inside, I don't care. But

make up your mind," he begged. "I'm being crushed under this weight!"

The mover couldn't hold on to the **heavy** crate any longer. He dropped it, and the paper wrapping ripped open. Hercule jumped on top of it and **YELLED** his battle cry:

"HERCULE POIRAT!"

He eagerly tore at the paper. "What kind of *surprise* will I find inside? I think I know what it is!"

"**NOOO!**" Aunt Bamboozle shrieked.
"*Yeees!*" Hercule squealed.
"*Ooohhh!*" I gasped.

Inside the enormouse box was not a machine to bottle the Bamboozle Bubbly Beverage, but a printing machine to make fake bills!

Hercule opened more of the crates. He discovered a machine to wash the counterfeit bills and another that looked like a hanging rack, to dry them. Another

crate was full of **PHONY MONEY**!

FURIOUS, Aunt Bamboozle began chasing my friend.

"You ruined my plans! I'll **SQUASH** your little mozzarella head!" she threatened. "I will shred you like a hunk of cheddar! I will boil you like a pot of spaghetti! I will slice you like a wheel of provolone!"

I knew I had to help my friend, but I was **no match** for her.

Instead, I appealed to her vanity.

"So are your nephews the brains behind the operation?" I asked her.

She stopped pummeling Hercule for a moment. "Are you kidding? I am the brains behind **Dr. Falsefur**! I am the genius who designs the bills and plans out how to distribute them. My nephews don't have the intelligence of a cheese curd! They couldn't do this on their own!"

Slow down! Heeelp! Get back here! Argh!

"I, Bettina Bamboozle, am the one true genius, Dr. Falsefur!"

A crowd had gathered at the sound of the commotion. She posed for pictures.

"That's right, it's me!" she said. "Take photos of me, not my cheesebrain nephews."

Balencio, Burton, and Bobo glared at her.

"If you want to take all the glory, Aunt, then take all the BLAME!" Balencio said.

Bettina bonked her three nephews on the head: Bonk! Bonk! Bonk!

"Quiet!" she commanded. "You never had a problem with me running things before. It was nice having all of that fake cash to spend, wasn't it?"

The three nephews squeaked, "Ouch! Ouch! Ouch!"

"And if you don't behave, I'll never cook for you again!" she threatened.

The three nephews sighed with relief.

"To tell the truth, Aunt Bettina, we don't like your cooking!" Burton confessed.

While they were arguing, Hercule called the police. Then he snickered at the nephews.

"Don't worry, gentlemice. Where the police will take you, your aunt will not be there to cook those fur-curdling recipes," he said.

Tears of **joy** ran down their faces.

"We're so happy!" the nephews agreed.

"We won't miss our aunt bonking our heads all the time, either," Balencio added.

The police arrived and pawcuffed Bettina Bamboozle.

"*Ungrateful!*" she howled. "You don't know anything about good cooking. But that makes sense. Nobody appreciates my genius!"

The police pawcuffed the nephews next.

"This will teach you all not to print fake money," Hercule told them. "In the end, honesty always wins!"

"That's right, my friend," I said. "I'm glad the **bad guys** didn't get away this time."

At that moment, a long leopard-print limo with tinted windows rolled down the street. Three **massive** rodents, as **massive** as a chest of drawers, got out of the car. They each carried a **leopard-print** suitcase. Determined and confident, they headed toward the Bamboozle house as if they had something very important to do.

The dark glass of the stretch limo rolled

down slowly, and the snout of a rodent **APPEARED** through the window.

It was *Madame No*!

What is she doing here? I wondered.

She looked in alarm at the scene. When she figured out that the Bamboozle Family had been caught, she called to her three assistants in a harsh WHISPER.

"Psssst . . . Stop! Come back!"

"But you told us to pick up the ca—" they squeaked.

She interrupted them. "Come back!"

"But the cash . . . the suitcases . . . the Bamboozles . . ." they **insisted**.

Now she was **furious**. "I said to come back!" she yelled. "And keep quiet! The whole thing is off!"

The three scrambled into the vehicle, and the limo took off as Madame No screamed, *"Geronimo, this is not the end! You'll pay for this!"*

"Interesting." Hercule chuckled. "It looks like Madame No was in cahoots with Bettina Bamboozle to pick up three suitcases of FAKE BILLS, but not anymore! Hee, hee, hee!"

BACK TO THE
GOLDEN CHEESE

My cousin Trap heard the news and showed up at my house.

"Great job cracking the case, Geronimo," he said. "Let's go back to the GOLDEN CHEESE to celebrate. Dinner's on you, my generous cousin. Happy, Geronimo?"

"Of course," I grumbled.

The police had just returned my **real** wallet and credit card, so I could pay. But . . .

Holey cheese! Couldn't he have chosen another place?

Huh?

Oops!

The news of the celebration spread quickly. When Trap, Hercule, and I got to the restaurant, my friends, family, and coworkers were waiting for us.

We dined on a seven-course meal of *whisker-licking* good cheese dishes! We had cheese soup, fried cheese sticks, cheese soufflé, cheese ravioli, cheeseburgers, cheese fondue, and cheese pizza. Then we finished with delicious cheesecake and assorted cheese shakes!

I enjoyed it so much when my *tummy* wasn't grumbling. It helped me forget how rotten my BIRTHDAY had been the day before!

When it was time to pay, the manager gave me the bill. I rummaged through my pockets for my wallet. I couldn't find it! I became red with EMBARRASSMENT.

Um . . .

My wallet?!

You see . . .

You forgot it?

"Um, well, I, actually, unfortunately, you won't believe this, but I can't pay. I lost my wallet!" I said.

The manager stared at me sternly. "You forgot your wallet, huh?" he grumbled. "Everybody says the same thing when they don't want to pay!"

The manager gave me an apron.

"Don't you worry, Mr. Stilton. You'll WASH all the dishes for a month. You can live here at the restaurant, and I'll release you when the bill is paid in full," he said.

I took the apron from him with a sigh. "Very well," I said. "I suppose I have no choice."

To my surprise, he burst out laughing. "It was a joke, Mr. Stilton. I thought you knew!"

You'll wash all the dishes!

Argh!

All my friends **BURST OUT LAUGHING**. They were all in on it! My cousin Trap **laughed** the hardest.

"I was a joke, Cousinkins!" he said. "I slipped your wallet out of your **pocket** when we were talking before.

I squeaked,

"HUHHHHHHHHHHHHHHHHH? WHAAAAAA!?"

My friends told me they were going to pay the bill, to make up for my bad birthday.

"Yes, that was one bamboozle of a BiRTHDAY," I said, laughing, and everyone laughed with me.

That's the SECRET of Mouse Island: No matter what happens, we never lose our sense of humor. Why?

Because laughter is like sunshine — it can brighten any day!

I give you my word: the word of Stilton, Geronimo Stilton!

A GOOD SENSE OF HUMOR IS THE SECRET OF MOUSE ISLAND!

HA, HA, HA!

Mosquitoes

Two mosquitoes went to a restaurant.

"What would you like to eat?" the waiter asked.

"The chef!" they answered.

Birds

Which bird is at every meal?

The swallow!

HEE, HEE, HEE!

Soccer

Why was the soccer ball angry?

It didn't like being kicked around all the time!

Rooster

If a rooster laid an egg on a roof, which way would it roll?

Nowhere — roosters don't lay eggs!

Eggs

Two farmers met at the corner store.

"Howdy! What's happening?" the first asked.

"My hen started laying golden eggs," the second farmer answered.

"That's amazing! You must be thrilled!" his friend said.

"No, it's terrible." the second farmer replied sadly. "I can't make a decent omelet anymore!"

HO, HO, HO!

Dragon

What does a dragon eat with cheese?

Firecrackers!

Snake

Why couldn't the snake talk?

He had a frog in his throat!

HO, HO, HO! HA, HA, HA!

Cows

What did the mommy cow say to the baby cow?

"It's pasture bedtime!"

Don't miss a single fabumouse adventure!

Up Next:

Visit Geronimo in every universe!

Spacemice

Geronimo Stiltonix and his crew are out of this world!

Cavemice

Geronimo Stiltonoot, an ancient ancestor, is friends with the dinosaurs in the Stone Age!

Micekings

Geronimo Stiltonord live amongst the dragons i the ancient far north!

THE *Geronimo Stilton* SERIES COMES TO LIFE IN A BRAND-NEW DIGITAL WORLD

MEET Geronimo and Thea Stilton—
and explore the *Geronimo Stilton* Island.
PLAY games, create an avatar, and chat with other fans.

Start your adventure today! Download the **HOME BASE** app and scan this image to unlock exclusive rewards!

SCHOLASTIC.COM/HOMEBASE

SCHOLASTIC

HBGERONIMOF19

Don't miss any of these exciting Thea Sisters adventures!

Thea Stilton and the Dragon's Code

Thea Stilton and the Mountain of Fire

Thea Stilton and the Ghost of the Shipwreck

Thea Stilton and the Secret City

Thea Stilton and the Mystery in Paris

Thea Stilton and the Cherry Blossom Adventure

Thea Stilton and the Star Castaways

Thea Stilton: Big Trouble in the Big Apple

Thea Stilton and the Ice Treasure

Thea Stilton and the Secret of the Old Castle

Thea Stilton and the Blue Scarab Hunt

Thea Stilton and the Prince's Emerald

Thea Stilton and the Mystery on the Orient Express

Thea Stilton and the Dancing Shadows

Thea Stilton and the Legend of the Fire Flowers

Thea Stilton and the Spanish Dance Mission

Thea Stilton and the Journey to the Lion's Den

Thea Stilton and the Great Tulip Heist

Thea Stilton and the Chocolate Sabotage

Thea Stilton and the Missing Myth

Thea Stilton and the Lost Letters

Thea Stilton and the Tropical Treasure

Thea Stilton and the Hollywood Hoax

Thea Stilton and the Madagascar Madness

Thea Stilton and the Frozen Fiasco

Thea Stilton and the Venice Masquerade

Thea Stilton and the Niagara Splash

Thea Stilton and the Riddle of the Ruins

Thea Stilton and the Phantom of the Orchestra

Thea Stilton and the Black Forest Burglary

Thea Stilton and the Race for the Gold

ABOUT THE AUTHOR

Born in New Mouse City, Mouse Island, **GERONIMO STILTON** is Rattus Emeritus of Mousomorphic Literature and of Neo-Ratonic Comparative Philosophy. For the past twenty years, he has been running *The Rodent's Gazette*, New Mouse City's most widely read daily newspaper.

Stilton was awarded the Ratitzer Prize for his scoops on *The Curse of the Cheese Pyramid* and *The Search for Sunken Treasure*. He has also received the Andersen 2000 Prize for Personality of the Year. One of his bestsellers won the 2002 eBook Award for world's best ratling's electronic book. His works have been published all over the globe.

In his spare time, Mr. Stilton collects antique cheese rinds and plays golf. But what he most enjoys is telling stories to his nephew Benjamin.

1. **Main entrance**
2. **Printing presses** (where the books and newspaper are printed)
3. **Accounts department**
4. **Editorial room** (where the editors, illustrators, and designers work)
5. **Geronimo Stilton's office**
6. **Helicopter landing pad**

THE RODENT'S
GAZETTE

Map of New Mouse City

1. Industrial Zone
2. Cheese Factories
3. Angorat International Airport
4. WRAT Radio and Television Station
5. Cheese Market
6. Fish Market
7. Town Hall
8. Snotnose Castle
9. The Seven Hills of Mouse Island
10. Mouse Central Station
11. Trade Center
12. Movie Theater
13. Gym
14. Catnegie Hall
15. Singing Stone Plaza
16. The Gouda Theater
17. Grand Hotel
18. Mouse General Hospital
19. Botanical Gardens
20. Cheap Junk for Less (Trap's store)
21. Aunt Sweetfur and Benjamin's House
22. Mouseum of Modern Art
23. University and Library
24. *The Daily Rat*
25. *The Rodent's Gazette*
26. Trap's House
27. Fashion District
28. The Mouse House Restaurant
29. Environmental Protection Center
30. Harbor Office
31. Mousidon Square Garden
32. Golf Course
33. Swimming Pool
34. Tennis Courts
35. Curlyfur Island Amousement Park
36. Geronimo's House
37. Historic District
38. Public Library
39. Shipyard
40. Thea's House
41. New Mouse Harbor
42. Luna Lighthouse
43. The Statue of Liberty
44. Hercule Poirat's Office
45. Petunia Pretty Paws's House
46. Grandfather William's House

Map of Mouse Island

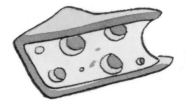

Dear mouse friends,
Thanks for reading, and farewell
till the next book.
It'll be another whisker-licking-good
adventure, and that's a promise!

Geronimo Stilton